C000135488

For Chris and Maureen
"The Odd Couple"

Once there was a cockatiel, *in love* with an Alsatian. To *her* the bird did not appeal. An *awkward* situation.

He always tried to win her heart. He would *not* give up!
He'd loved her from the very start – since when she was a
pup.

He'd comb his fuzzy yellow crest then trim his shiny claws.

Chew minty gum, puff out his chest and *try* to kiss her paws.

He'd wear his dinky bow tie and wash each rosy cheek.
He'd buy the best that seed could buy – hold roses in his
beak.

He'd watch her from the curtain pole then ring his little bell.

He'd scoop her food *into* her bowl and quite *enjoyed* the smell.

When it was her bath time, he'd land upon the tap...

but if she saw him – out she'd climb and then he'd *have* to flap!

She'd chase him *all around* the place until she'd stop to drink
and when they would come face to face – he'd give a cheeky wink.

She *nearly* ate him now and then – lots of near misses,
and when it happened once again, he said, "she's blowing
kisses."

He *always* tried to dance with her, he longed for her affection.

He loved her eyes, her size and fur. He felt a *deep* connection.

The time then came to take the chance and try out a *new* plan.
To win his girl, have love, romance, he *had* to be her man.

He flew upon the door frame, where it was cold and dark but he stayed there all the same then *screeched* a *mighty* BARK!

She ran straight to the kitchen door, excited but confused. She looked up high then sniffed the floor. He was *quite* amused!

She thought she'd found her *dream* dog then but she
needed proof.
"Woof!" he shouted once again... "Woof! Woof! Woof!
Woof! *WOOF!*"

She *had* to meet her hidden love. She could not wait to see.
His voice echoed from *high* above. What kind of dog *was* he?
She stood up tall against the wall – turned on the kitchen
light
but didn't see a *dog* at all – a rather *different* sight.

She saw the cheeky cockatiel – just as he'd always been. She sighed but then began to feel, she *had* been *rather* mean.

"You are a *little* sweet," she said. "My knight in shining armour."

He flew down then and kissed her head. A *proper* little charmer.

Off she ran and off he flew. She now loves *every* feather. He smirked because he always knew – that they would be together. It doesn't matter *what* you are, it's just a simple fact – *high* or low and near or far – opposites *attract!*

Hayley Edwards

Silly Scribbles ltd

"You're sure to get the giggles!

Printed in Great Britain
by Amazon